7

The Raft

JIM LAMARCHE

THE RAFT

HarperCollins*Publishers*

The Raft

Copyright © 2000 by Jim LaMarche

Printed in Hong Kong by South China Printing Company (1988) Ltd.

All rights reserved.

http://www.harperchildrens.com

LIBRARY OF CONGRESS CATALOGING-IN-PUBLICATION DATA

LaMarche, Jim. The raft/Jim LaMarche. p. cm.

Summary: Reluctant Nicky spends a wonderful summer with Grandma,

who introduces him to the joy of rafting down the river near her home

and watching the animals along the banks.

ISBN 0-688-13977-9 (trade)—ISBN 0-688-13978-7 (library)

[1. Grandmothers—Fiction.   2. Rafting (Sports)—Fiction.

3. Rivers—Fiction.   4. Animals—Fiction.]   I. Title.

PZ7.L15957Raf 2000   [E]—dc21   99-35546   CIP

10 9 8 7 6 5 4 3 2 1

❖

First Edition

For Susan Pearson
Thanks for your help through the bends
and shallows

A Note from the Author

THIS STORY IS LIKE THE CIGAR BOX I kept as a boy—it's full of bits and pieces of my boyhood summers.

Like Nicky in *The Raft*, I spent those summers with my grandparents at a cottage in the north woods. My grandma was a self-taught artist and a fine fryer of perch and bluegill.

Also like Nicky, I once found an old raft. It happened one day when my dad and I were running our dog, Brownie, in the rolling hills near town. We came to an abandoned camp, where we found a small artesian pond with water coming up from underground springs as cold and clear as glass. In the weeds along the shore, we found an old raft and a smooth pine pole. Much to my surprise, my dad let me take the raft out on the pond by myself.

And again like Nicky, I discovered the power of drawing, and learned that when you draw something, you get closer to it and know it better.

This story is a little about all of those things—a summer in the woods, a special grandparent, becoming a river rat, and becoming an artist.

T HERE'S NOBODY TO PLAY WITH," I complained. "She doesn't even have a TV."

Dad grinned. "Well, she's not your normal kind of grandma, I guess," he said. "Calls herself a river rat." He chuckled. "But I promise, she'll find plenty for you to do. And you know I can't take you with me this summer, Nicky. There'll be no kids there, and I'll be spending all my time at the plant."

I felt tears starting again, but I blinked hard and looked out the window.

That afternoon, I stood in Grandma's yard

and watched my dad drive away. Dust rose up

behind our car as it disappeared into the pines.

"Well, we can't stand here all summer," said

Grandma. "C'mon, Nicky, it's time for supper."

"Honey or maple syrup on your cornbread?" Grandma asked.

"I don't like cornbread," I mumbled, poking my finger into the syrup pitcher when she wasn't looking.

"If you're going to do that, you'd better wash up first," she said. She had eyes in the back of her head. "Bathroom's through there."

I pushed the doorway curtain aside and walked into what would have been a living room in anyone else's house. Books were scattered everywhere—on the tables, on the chairs, even on the floor. Three of the walls were cluttered with sketches and stuffed fish and charts of the river. Several fishing poles hung from the fourth with a tackle box, a snorkle, and a mask on the floor beneath them. It looked like a river rat's workroom, all right, except that in the middle of everything was a half-finished carving of a bear.

"Been carving that old fellow for years," Grandma called from the kitchen. "The real one hangs out at the dump. Now come get your supper, before I feed it to him."

Dad was right—Grandma found plenty for me to do. In the morning, I stacked firewood, then helped her clean out the rain gutters and change the spark plugs on her truck. The afternoon was almost over when she handed me a cane pole, a bobber, and some red worms.

"Fish fry tonight!" she said, showing me how to bait the hook. "That river's full of fat bluegills. Drop your line near the lily pads and you'll find 'em."

Down at the dock, I looked things over. The lily pads were too close to shore. There couldn't be fish there. I walked to the end of the dock and threw my line out as far as I could. Then I sat down to wait. And wait. And wait. My bobber never moved.

"There's no fish in this stupid river," I said out loud, disgusted.

We had hamburgers for supper.

"Give it another try," said Grandma the next evening. "I'll bet you catch something."

Don't count on it, I thought, as I headed back to the dock. I threw my line in the water. Then I stretched out on the dock to wait. I must have fallen asleep, because I was awakened by loud chirping and chattering. I sat up and looked around. A flock of birds was moving toward me along the river, hovering over something floating on the water. It drifted downstream, closer and closer, until finally it bumped up against the dock.

Though it was covered with leaves and branches, now I could tell that it was a raft. What was it doing floating down the river all by itself, I wondered. I reached down and pushed some of the leaves aside. Beneath them was a drawing of a rabbit. It looked like those ancient cave paintings I'd seen in books—just outlines, but wild and fast and free.

I cleaned away more leaves and it was like finding presents under the Christmas tree. A bear, a fox, a raccoon—all with the wild look of the rabbit. Who had drawn them, I wondered. Where had the raft come from?

I ran up to the cottage. Grandma was on the porch, reading.

"Do you have some rope I can use?" I asked.

"In the shed, hon," she said. "Help yourself." She didn't ask me what I needed it for, and I decided not to tell her yet.

I pushed the raft into the reeds along the river's edge, then tied it to the dock so it wouldn't drift away. All the while, birds flew over my head, every now and then swooping down to the raft as if it were a friend. A crane waded through the reeds to it. A turtle swam up from the bottom of the river.

The moon had risen yellow over the river by the time I went up to the cottage to go to bed.

I was already down at the dock the next morning when Grandma appeared with a life jacket and a long pole. She didn't seem surprised by the raft at all, or by the animal pictures all over it.

"How did you know . . . ?" I started.

"Let's go," Grandma interrupted, tossing me the life jacket and stepping onto the raft. She pushed the pole hard into the river bottom and we moved smoothly into the current.

"Your turn," she said after a few minutes. She showed me how to hold the pole and push, and I poled us to the middle of the river. Even there, the water wasn't over my head.

We poled the raft up the river, then let it slowly drift back down. The birds kept us company the whole time, soaring, swooping, singing. Some even landed on the raft and rode with us for a while. Hitchhikers, Grandma called them.

After that, I had little time for anything but the raft. I raced through whatever chores there were, then ran down to the dock, wondering what animals I'd see that day.

It wasn't just birds that the raft attracted. One morning three raccoons followed me along the shore. Another time a turtle climbed on board and spent the morning sunning itself. And one afternoon I saw a family of foxes slip through the trees along the river.

When the weather turned too hot and sticky to
sleep indoors, Grandma helped me put up a small
tent on the raft. I lay on top of the cool sheets and
read comic books by flashlight until I fell asleep. One
night, a noise woke me up. There in the moonlight
stood a huge buck. He looked right at me, then
lowered his head to drink, as if I wasn't there at all.

I found Grandma the next morning working on
her bear carving.

"Do you have some extra paper I could draw on?"
I asked her.

She brought out a big sketchpad and a pouch
filled with thick pencils and crayons. "I've been
saving these just for you," she said. "Better take these,
too." She held out the snorkle and mask. "Never
know when they might come in handy on a raft."

The sun was hot that afternoon, so I poled into the shade of a willow, then waited to see what animals the raft would bring. It wasn't long before a great blue heron whooshed down with a crayfish in its bill.

I grabbed a pencil and began to sketch. I felt invisible as the bird calmly ate its lunch right in front of me. Then it preened its feathers, looked back up the river, and flew off.

That night I showed my drawing to Grandma.

"Not bad," she said. "Not bad at all!" And she tacked it on the wall on top of one of her own sketches.

One day I poled upriver farther than I'd ever been. Near a clump of tall cattails, I startled an otter family. They dove underwater, but, as with the other animals, the raft seemed to calm them down. Soon they were playing all around me.

Grandma had been right about the mask and snorkel coming in handy. I slipped them on, then hung my head over the raft and watched the otters play—chasing fish, chasing each other, sometimes just chasing their own tails. I kept very still, but they didn't seem to mind me watching. They played keep away with a small stone, then tug-of-war with a piece of rope. It was like they were showing off for me. They even let me feed them right out of my hand.

Some mornings, Grandma would make a bagful of sandwiches and a thermos of icy lemonade. Then we'd put on our bathing suits, grab some towels, a lawn chair, and an inner tube, and pole upriver to her favorite swimming spot. "I've come swimming here since I was a girl," she told me as we tied the raft to an old dock. "The Marshalls used to live here—all ten of them. What a herd of wild animals we were!"

While Grandma watched from the inner tube, I practiced my flying cannonballs. Then we'd eat our lunch, and she'd tell me stories about growing up on the river. My favorite was of the time she'd found a small black pearl inside a river clam. "I still have it," she said.

Somehow, on the river, it seemed like summer would never end. But of course it did.

On my last day, I got up extra early and crept down to the dock. The air was cool and a low pearly fog hung over the river. I untied the raft and quietly drifted downstream.

Ahead of me, through the fog, I saw two deer moving across the river, a doe and her fawn. When they reached the shore, the doe leaped easily up the steep bank, then turned to wait for her baby. But the fawn was in trouble. It kept slipping down the muddy bank. The doe returned to the water to help, but the more the fawn struggled, the deeper it got stuck in the mud.

I pushed off the river bottom and drove the raft hard onto the muddy bank, startling the doe. Then I dropped into the water. I was ankle-deep in mud.

"You're okay," I whispered to the fawn, praying that the raft would calm it. "I won't hurt you."

Gradually the fawn stopped struggling, as if it understood that I was there to help. I put my arms around it and pulled. It barely moved. I pulled again, then again. Slowly the fawn eased out of the mud, and finally it was free. Carefully I carried the fawn up the bank to its mother.

Then, quietly, I returned to the raft. From there, I watched the doe nuzzle and clean her baby, and I knew what I had to do. I pulled the stub of a crayon from my pocket, and drew the fawn, in all its wildness, onto the old gray boards of the raft. When I had finished, I knew it was just right.

After supper, I showed Grandma my drawing of the fawn and told her my story.

"It's perfect," she said, "but we need to do one more thing." She hurried up to the cottage. When she came back, she had tubes of oil paint and two brushes.

Grandma helped me trace my drawing with the oil paint, which soaked deep into the wood. "That'll keep it," she said. "Now you'll always be part of the river."

"Just like you, Grandma," I told her. "A river rat."

Grandma laughed. "Just like me," she agreed.